Once apun a Time

by
Cory Marx
and
Miles Beck

Once aPun a Time

This book is a work of fiction. Names, characters, businesses, organizations, places, events, and incidents either are the product of the author's imagination or are used fictitiously. Any resemblance to actual persons, living or dead, events or locales is entirely coincidental.

First Edition

ISBN 978-0-9845849-0-1

Printed in the United States of America

9 8 7 6 5 4 3 2 1

Cover Design: Cory Marx

Dedication

We dedicate this book to
all the trees that had died for its cause.

Keeping Worm

chapter 1

So my friend just gave me tickets to my least favorite NBA team, so now I need to *Celtics*.

—◊—

Did you hear about that space football player? Yea, he just *Touch Down*.

—◊—

So did you hear about the international cross country celebration? It was quite a *Race*.

—◊—

What did the teenager who went to the NFL eat?
Pro-tein

—◊—

What's a dwarf's favorite type of math?
Trigo-NOMEtry

—◊—

How do dwarf's stay in rhythm while dancing?
They use a metro-NOME

How did the Mexican skeleton launch the arrow?
With El-bow

—w—

What did the Jamaican miner say when he got trapped?
I'm a Diamond!

—w—

What is a landscaper's favorite Disney movie?
Mow-lawn

—w—

What do Eskimo's use to hold their houses together?
I-glue

—w—

What is a bird's favorite part of the human body?
The Pecks

—w—

What is a cow's favorite Disney movie?
Moo-lan

What announcement did the emcee yell that made everyone leave the concert?
"A-band-on!"

—◊—

Where did Noah play in his free time?
Arc-ade

—◊—

What makes the band, "Foot & Sock", a good band?
They can Toe Jam.

—◊—

I like *Ma-gellan* techniques; They always glue me in to where I'm going.

—◊—

It seems no matter where you go in the South, there's always a swamp *Bayou*.

My holiday tree has been in the garage all year; some *ChristMOSS* started growing on it.

—◊—

What's important to have while going on a running quest? Jour-Knee

—◊—

When I went to pay for my duck, I decided I didn't want it, cuz the *Bill* was too big.

—◊—

When they built my house, I was put into a wall. Now I'm *Stucco*.

—◊—

Pollution is creating a *Mess-osphere* in the sky.

—◊—

The congregation at the Pope's funeral is going to be *Mass-ive*.

So this one-eyed pirate asked his captain, "Which communication device should I use?" And he's like, "*Dis-patch*".

—⚬—

What do you need to hit an electronic baseball?
A Bat-tery

—⚬—

Who's Santa Clause's favorite singer?
Elf-is

—⚬—

What's a dog's favorite root beer?
Barks

—⚬—

What's a car's favorite drink?
En-gin-ger-ale

What type of house does a gingerbread live in?

A Con-dough

—∞—

What did Miley Cyrus say when she got the same bad hand twice in the game, Uno? "Dang, not this *Card-igan*!" (Party in the U.S.A.)

—∞—

I always cook food around Christmas time, its *tra-Dishin.*

—∞—

What is toilet paper's favorite type of math?

Multi-Ply

—∞—

So I was shopping at this Zoo gift shop complex, and some tiger *Mall-ed* me...

What's a rancher's favorite math?
Cow-culous

—w—

Whenever I *Rome, I-taly* how many times I eat pasta.

—w—

What type of detergent does the ocean use?
Tide

—w—

What did the horse say to the rancher when the horse was thrown in jail?
"Hay,-Bail me out!"

—w—

What do you need to *begin* making clothes?
START-cchhh

—w—

What's an iPod's favorite dance move?
Shuffle

How many ducks are needed for them to get sleepy?
A Bill-yaaaaawn

—ɯ—

What brand of gangsta clothes does a bat wear while flying into a never-ending cave?
Echo Unltd.

—ɯ—

I thought up a utensil joke, but I *Fork-ot* it.

—ɯ—

I would make fun of cross county, but I've *Run* out of jokes...

—ɯ—

My house used to be shallow, but after I visited the hardware store, my *Home Depot.*

—ɯ—

Yeah, some appliances stores have their highs, and some have their *Lowe's.*

When I touched my computer chip, it was *Micro-soft*.

—⁓—

Even after I *changed* the ingredients to the recipe, my friend still said that he'd *Edit*.

—⁓—

What type of animal cooks rice in what?
A Pan...duuuh!

—⁓—

I always know when Santa has come, I can sense his *Presents*.

—⁓—

Who's a medieval night's favorite basketball player?
Pao Castle

—⁓—

I'm going to Dana Point harbor, *Yachta* come.

What did the hungry donkey say when it got cold?
Burrrr-ito

What do you call a table made out of carrots?
A vege-Table

What do you call a really old telephone pole?
A Volt-Age

The city of *Pear-is* kind of fruity.

My horse got stung by a bee, I bet that *Mustang*.

Sometimes I can *Bear*ly survive the great outdoors.

Why did the baker rob the bank?

For the Dough

—⚬—

What does the Baker use to open his restaurant?

A Cook-key

—⚬—

What does the Baker use to cool off his treats?

The Wind-Dough

—⚬—

So I saw a sign on the glass at the casino, it said I could *Win-Dow*.

—⚬—

What do you need to enter the underwater hotel?

A Reservoir-tion

What do you call someone who steals ice?

A Roburrr

—✺—

The Real-estate agent said the way I write consonants wasn't too good, so I should try to use *Proper-T's...*

—✺—

Why couldn't the Royalty breathe?

He had no Heir

—✺—

Why didn't the King get away with the crime?

They found his Prince

—✺—

Where did the doctor tell the anxious person to go? The hospital, cuz everyone there's *Patient.*

What did Sam-I-Am say went he went to Japan?
Sam-er-i

—◇—

What did the Australian runner say when he saw his
Chinese friend?
Wanna have a Race?

—◇—

What do you call an environmental bunch of criminals that
get infections?
Gang-Green

—◇—

What did the sheep say when its collar was running away?
Stay-Bell!

—◇—

What did the baker say when his teacher asked him a hard
question?
I *Doughn't* know.

What's a bird's favorite type of nuts?

Pecan

—◊—

So I went to this humorous band concert yesterday. They played *Symphony* stuff...

—◊—

I heard some guy tried to hang himself but the knot broke. That's such good *Neuce*.

—◊—

So this bearded golfer kept bragging about how good he was. And I was like, "Shut up and *Go-tee*!"

—◊—

What happened to the hand who bought something with the five-finger discount?

He was *Awristed*.

What do you call an evil Jamaican spice harvester?
A Cinnamon

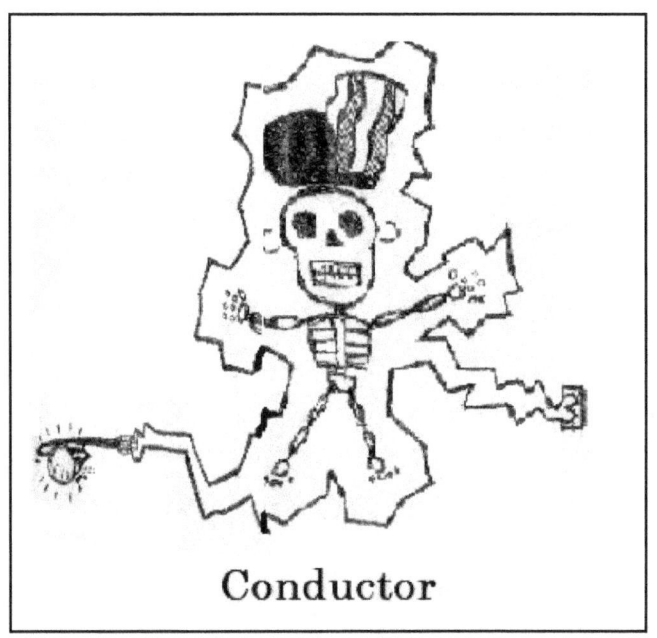

Conductor

chapter 2

Like a powerful emperor, this book is *Wide-Ruled*.

―∿―

I'll bring the queen food, *Em-Pour-her* a drink.

―∿―

What is the moon's favorite type of gum?
Orbit

―∿―

Did you see the documentary about feet? It had some pretty good *Foot-age.*

―∿―

My friend has a pretty fruity profession, he's a *Plum-er.*

―∿―

How do mermaids get their tails so shiny?
They use Sea-quins

Joseph Smiths' brother was looking for a job, but nobody wanted to *Hyrum*...

—⚭—

The crying baby finally went to sleep today; it was good *Snews*.

—⚭—

I can't figure out how to open my new cologne bottle. It doesn't make any *Scents*.

—⚭—

Why don't trees ever get lost?
They always stick to their Routes

—⚭—

Why don't trees ever reach their destination during the Winter?
Because they never Leaf.

—⚭—

I *Winder* if the Chicago Bulls win-D a lot.

This past semester with BP, I went through a lot of *Term-Oil.*

—⚡—

Which Lord of the Rings character always runs out of arrows?
Arrow-Gone

—⚡—

When you buy nuts at the store, they always *Cashew.*

—⚡—

So I went to the cattle ranch/driving school to learn how to *Steer.*

—⚡—

What do critic ghosts say?
Boo!

What did the food critic say when he entered the dirty food market?
"This place looks Grocer than usual."

—⁓—

What are a bad Jack-o-lanterns' kids called?
Punk-Kin

—⁓—

What do you call an Elephant who specializes in skin care?
A Pacoderm-atoligist

—⁓—

Why couldn't the prison escapee ever pass English class?
He could never finish his sentence

—⁓—

What kind of gum does Poseidon chew?
Trident

—⁓—

The ground has a lot of cracks in it; do you think that they *Cement* to do that?

My coffee table drink holder is pretty exciting, like a *Roller-coaster.*

—⁓—

What is the wealthiest bird?

The Ost-Rich

—⁓—

While I was transporting vegetables, my tire blew out. I will have to use *A-Spare-I-Guess.*

—⁓—

Why did the blueprint for the fish school weigh so much?

Because it was drawn to Scale

—⁓—

Did you hear about the cow who tried to assassinate the field? It's okay though, he only *Grazed* him.

When I get rich, I'm going to buy all of the oxygen. Then I'll be a *Million-air.*

—∿—

What do Newscasters do when they can't read the teleprompter?
They Improve-Eyes

—∿—

What do feet attack with during Christmas?
Missile-Toes

—∿—

What does a male doctor get in his free time?
A Man-i-Cure

—∿—

Why can't art collectors create their own art?
Because they have Poor-Traits

What did the sailors on the Titanic use to wash their hands?
The Sink

—◊—

Why do girls go to Yellowstone?
Because that's where all the Geyser.

—◊—

So a shaving razor was holding my sister hostage, and I'm like, "*Gillette* her go?!"

—◊—

Why are airplane operators so unhealthy?
Because they eat Pie-lots

—◊—

They just re-paved this street. I'm so happy to *Avenue* road!

—◊—

Wow, this type of European hotel is a pretty *Swed-edish Inn.*

What did the slow diamond polisher say to the others who were leaving?
"Can't *Jewel* wait up for me?"

—◊—

I love running in cold races... I *Winter* who will come in first.

—◊—

Did you hear about the competition where you're not allowed to use your muscles?
Yeah, well the guy who won got *Atrophy*.

—◊—

At my wig shop there are many ways *Toupee*.

—◊—

What did the early Europeans use to make their doors swivel?
A Stone-Hinge.

What do you call dwarfs who travel across the dessert?
Gnome-ads

—⚡—

I just saw a really short man walking around, does anyone *Gnome*?

—⚡—

I was so happy when I bought butter the other day; I got it for *Marginal*...cost.

—⚡—

This woman is very dehydrated, please don't *Ne-gate-oer-ade.*

—⚡—

Why was the college graduation so hot?
Because there were too many degrees.

—⚡—

My friend was cheating in golf, but I decided to play the *Fairway.*

Whenever I bake, I always listen to *Beeth-oven.*

—⁓—

In the Lord of the Rings battle scenes music, there is always much *Violins.*

—⁓—

So this mountain climber was talking about his trip, and he's like, "OK, let me *Summit* up for you..."

—⁓—

So one dolphin says to the other, "You know I can communicate with sound?" And the other one is like, "Dude! That's *So-Nar!*"

—⁓—

What did the manager of the knife manufacturing company say to his employees
"Looks like you have your work cut out for you."

—⁓—

"You need to count all of that chocolate?!" "Hmmm... I would just *Fudge* the numbers."

What do you call a brand of fruit that has lost a war?
Concord Grapes

—✳—

A soldier must have a lot of armor in his *War-drobe.*

—✳—

What is a police car made out of?
Copper

—✳—

What is a burglar's car made out of?
Steal

—✳—

"I sold all of my bracelets. I don't have any *Excess,-sorry.*"

—✳—

Where does a baby cow go to eat?
The Calf-eteria

Version 1:

This knight just moved from California to the North Pole, he's now called *Excali-Burr.*

—∿—

Version 2:

This knight figured out a way to put swords inside bullets, he's calling it the *"Ex-Caliber"*.

—∿—

Why aren't CEOs ever lonely?
Because they always have Company

—∿—

Where does the diamond polisher go to exercise?
The Gem

—∿—

So this priest collapsed in the middle of his sermon and I'm like, "Is there a *Doctrine* here?"

What did the parents say to the firefighter who was carrying their child out of a burning forest?
"Hey! That's Arson!"

—∞—

Where does a rancher go to get medicine?
A Farmacy

—∞—

Most people think that all boom boxes play music, but that's a *Stereotype.*

—∞—

What is a funny spy's favorite element?
Silly-Con

—∞—

Why did Osama Bin Laden have such a healthy heart?
Because he's Aerobic

—∞—

So I opened up a shop where people can buy skin samples, but nothing will *Cell....*

What part did the fruit sing in the choir?
Berry-Tone

—∾—

What emotion did the fruit have when it hit the wrong note in choir?
I'm-Berry-Sing

—∾—

How did Quazzi Motto know that the bishop was up to something?
He had a Hunch

—∾—

I had this idea for a new way to clean your teeth, but there were too many *Flaws*.

—∾—

People are saying that there is all of this water underground, WELL I don't know about that...

My friend sells pots for a living. He *Urns* some pretty good money.

—◊—

So my buddy is like, "Have you seen my farm land yet?" and I'm like, "Yeah man I just *Pasture* barn!"

—◊—

Whenever I go to an acoustic oil warehouse, I always *Guitar*.

—◊—

What type of water makes you feel bouncy?
Spring water

—◊—

A pitcher's job may seem pretty glamorous, but it really doesn't *aMound* to anything.

—◊—

What kind of machine only costs five cents?
A Mecha-Nickel one.

What did Columbus say when he found land across the Atlantic?
"It's A-merical!"

—w—

What does an orange tree do when listens to music?
It Groves...

—w—

Why was the Irish warrior such a manly warrior?
He was never Kilt...

—w—

What Roman emperor had lots of health issues?
Caesar

—w—

What is a film director's favorite type of spice?
Cinema-n

—w—

I was just released from court, so now I'm free, *In-a-Sense...*

So this one cop radios to another, "I just got the answers for the training exam." ...... *"Copy that."*

—◊—

The baking competition isn't very *Oven*-tful so far. I'm not *Pots*-itive that it will get better, but we'll see how the rest of it *Pans* out. But, *Boil* it be fun if it goes well.

—◊—

I've been dating this navy girl for a long time now. I'm thinking about *Mariner.*

—◊—

What sport is the loudest?
Tennis! Because of all the Racket

—◊—

So this tyrannical king was just *Throne* out of his castle.

—◊—

What do you call it when an orthodontist makes a mistake?
acci-Dental

Wow! that button on the front of his house is *A-Door-a-Bell.*

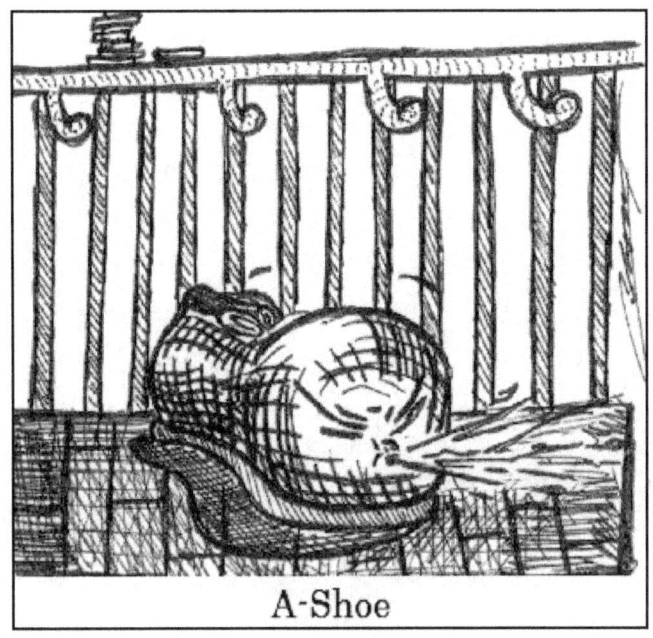

A-Shoe

chapter 3

My letter from a frog wouldn't open, so I had to *Ribbet*.

—⁄⁄⁄—

I had the hotel greeter park my car down the mountain in the *Valet*.

—⁄⁄⁄—

What plant is the best listener?
Corn, because of all its ears!

—⁄⁄⁄—

None of the other vacation spots were vacant, so I guess this is my last *Resort...*

—⁄⁄⁄—

My friend's favorite resort is a casino, where he has *Pair-a-Dice*.

—⁄⁄⁄—

What did the kid say when he was scammed at the fake carnival?
"That's not Fair!"

Where does the baseball catcher eat his food?
His Plate

—m—

I asked the airport employee where I could measure my luggage, and she's like, "*Weigh* over there."

—m—

Where do broken trains meet up?
The Junk-tion

—m—

Don't blame me for the earthquake in your city, it wasn't my *Fault.*

—m—

How did the zoo animal get into the army?
It was Giraff-ted

—m—

So the hot air in my car was making fun of me, and I'm like "Stop being a *Heater!*"

As opposed to common belief, to work at a salon, you *Mustach-ualy* grow hair above your mouth...

—ɯ—

What do you call a snail who shops a lot?
A Mall-usk

—ɯ—

What's a singer's favorite Juice drink?
High C

—ɯ—

What's a computer's favorite fast food restaurant?
Dell, Taco

—ɯ—

What's a computer's favorite fast food restaurant?
MACdonald's

—ɯ—

I was wondering what to train for in Cross Country, then my friend told me that endurance is better in the *Long Run*.

What did the French caveman say when he was done eating on top of a tower?
"I-Full"

—⟋⟍—

So lately I've been reflecting on mirrors...

—⟋⟍—

I can tell this baby is going to be good at basketball, he's already *Dribbling*.

—⟋⟍—

Okay, so there were these kids fighting over a waffle on a beach in California, then they dropped it. Now it's a *SanDy-eggo*...

—⟋⟍—

Hopefully you didn't waste any of your money at that fake cellular device store; it's a *Phoney*.

—⟋⟍—

Who is the most charitable singer?
Cher

What type of clothes play music at night?
Pa-Jammas

—~~—

The president of Egypt wasn't being so *Fair-o*...

—~~—

We don't know what caused the lung cancer, but we're
trying *Asbestos* we can to find out...

—~~—

So this ninja was just *Spine* on his chiropractor...

—~~—

So I *Coupon* getting these discounts in the mail...

—~~—

What is the quietest marine life?
Fishhhhhh...

So these two attorneys were *Lawyer-tering* in an empty court room and ones like, "It's *Just-Us*?"

—⫶—

What is a blackboard's favorite candy?
Chalk-olate

—⫶—

I thought that the wheels on my bike were fixed, but maybe I *Spoke* too soon...

—⫶—

I did not really like my performance, but some people cheered, so I guess that is
a-Plause.

—⫶—

How do you get steps to become huge?
You give them *Stair-oids*

—⫶—

You shouldn't be sleepy when you're standing near a cliff... but you *Can-Yawn*.

Why are beaches never lonely?
Because they always have Peers

—ɯ—

The doctor said I should rest my foot, *An-kle* it down with some ice.

—ɯ—

If you hurt someone *In-Jury*, you'll be guilty.

—ɯ—

Out of the entire art gallery, I *Picture* painting.

—ɯ—

So I thought of this *Hill-arious* mountain joke...

—ɯ—

So that mission to Mars didn't go very well... next time I think they should *Planet* better...

Those naughty hornets should *Bee-Hive*...

—⁓—

So my tree finally started to fill out this spring, that's such a *Re-Leaf*.

—⁓—

I had a dream that we all had to connect our letters when we write; that would be a *Curse-if* we had to do that.

—⁓—

What do bowling employees do when they lose benefits? They Strike

—⁓—

I need to *Rash-en* my allergy medication.

—⁓—

What did the priest say when he was asked to give a speech? "Ser-mon"

What did the head officer say when he was asked to catch a bandit?

"Sherr-if I have the time..."

—※—

I didn't room for your spare, so *Wheel* have to *Tires* on the roof...

—※—

I'm thinking about selling my dog some tennis balls, they'd probably *Fetch* a good price.

—※—

What did the gangsta investigator say when the sugar melted in water?

"Dis-Solved!"

—※—

What part of the planet is scariest?

At-Most-Fear

Priests must be pretty wealthy, from all their *Rich-uals*...

—⟆—

So this rabbit from California was giving a royal *decree* (about temperature) and he's like, "*Hair* ye *hair* ye, look to the East, the *Air-iz-on-a* higher temperature."

—⟆—

So this grizzly and a male cow were starting to fight. It was *Un-Bear-a-Bull* to watch.

—⟆—

In Baseball, you don't need to chew sunflowers to *Suck-Seed*.

—⟆—

My boat is getting pretty old... I'm thinking about *Saaaaiiiiiling* it.

—⟆—

My friend wouldn't eat his cake because it was purple; I'm like, "*Vio-let* the color stop you?"

I've been visiting my friend Frodo every week now, out of *Hobbit*.

—※—

I've been researching river mammals lately... but anyways I *Otter* get to bed, *Beaver* it gets too late.

—※—

What do you need to catch a lawyer fish?
De-Bait

—※—

What did the Pilgrim say at the desert table?
"Is there Pie-on-eer?"

—※—

So the mayor was *a-Warden* the prison manager for doing such an *ex-Cell-ent* job. I was *Jail-ous*.

—※—

The farmer's outfit looks pretty good..... *Overall*

What did the Cruise ship performer take to not be nervous?
Drama-mine

—◊—

What's ghost ninja's favorite plant?
Bam!-Boo!!

—◊—

Why do trees stretch a lot?
To keep Lumber

—◊—

I was going to join the Jamaican bobsled team... but my name didn't make the *Rasta*.

—◊—

I just got this perforated paper. It's *Terrible*.

—◊—

What does a drug-addict sleep on?
A Pill-ow

So these condiments were running from the cops and one asks, "Do you think they'll *Ketchup*?" and the other's like, "I don't even think they *Sauce*."

—⫘—

We should have *Plant* this garden better...

—⫘—

My friend was bragging about how he could catch fish with his bare hands, and I was like, "Get *Reel*!"

—⫘—

So the total income of a trash man before taxes is pretty *Gross*...

—⫘—

So I just made some *Graffiti* about my foot...

—⫘—

I'm pretty *Exit-ed* about leaving.

Why was the chemist suspended from school?
He always Toxin class

—⁂—

What is a rabbits' favorite metal?
Gold, because of all the carrots

—⁂—

Why did the lion eat the librarian?
Because Reader's Digest

—⁂—

Why did the baker put oil on the pan?
Because Breadsticks

—⁂—

I sure hope this protein is Creatine some muscles...

—⁂—

I was going to steal some steroids but my priest said it isn't good for Muscle...

What position in church goes to the mall a lot?
The Buy-shop

—〰—

What is a golfer's favorite drink?
Tee....

—〰—

That call I made 24 hours ago is now a Di-aled number.

—〰—

My all-time favorite board game is battleship. I *Warship* it.

—〰—

I didn't think there would be much open seating, but there's a *Bench* of it.

—〰—

I've never driven a plane before, so I guess I'm just going to have to *Wing* it...

My corn army buddy just got promoted to *Kernel...*

—⁕—

You know that one pharaoh? Yeah, *Egypt* me off!

—⁕—

Wire these chords being so lame?

—⁕—

How did the open window get into the army?

Through the Draft

—⁕—

What is a fence's favorite dance?

The Wall-tz

—⁕—

What did the cop do on his break?

He took Arrest.

Why do gangstas play golf?
So they can hit the club.

—⚉—

My boat broke, so I guess I'm going to have to *River-t* to swimming... I guess I'm just *un-Lake-y*...

—⚉—

The blood I gave yesterday went bad, so I guess it was all in *Vein*...

—⚉—

They wrote down the wrong blood type I have. It was a *Type-O*.

—⚉—

What is a doctors' favorite planet?
Mer-Cure-y

—⚉—

What is a baseball players' favorite bird?
Pitch-en

I went hunting in space. Now I have some Venus-en...

—⚡—

What is a Warrior's favorite gum?
Spear-mint

—⚡—

So I made a *College* of all the Universities I've attended...

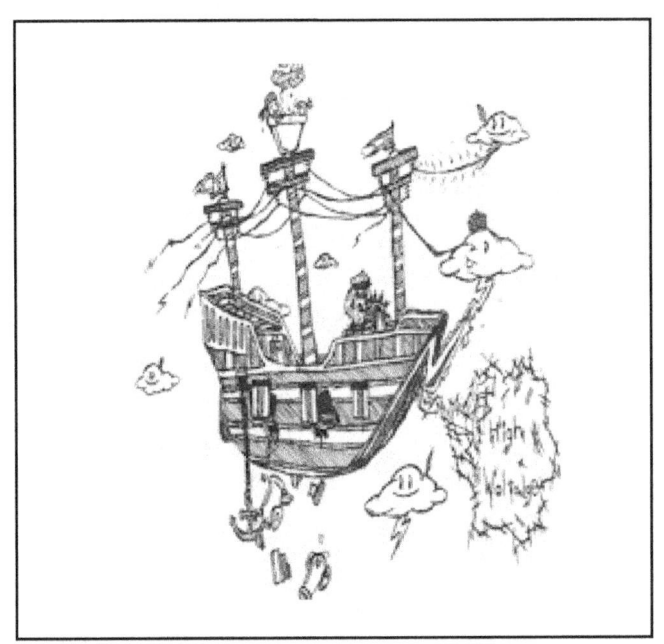

chapter 4

What does this book and gum have in common?
They're both in Mint Condition

—◦—

Did you hear about that cereal battle? Yeah, well *Fiber One*.

—◦—

I wasn't sure how many people to invite...so I *Guest*...

—◦—

My car *Fuels* like it needs some oil, but I'm just *Gas-ing*...

—◦—

Did you hear about that flying knight? Yeah, he *Sword*.

—◦—

So I was taking *Notes* in my music class...

—◦—

Why didn't the cargo want to travel in the boat?
It was a Freight

I usually carry extra pens in my pocket, just *Ink-Case*...

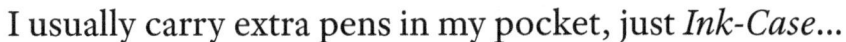

Why do gangstas like it when people's car batteries die?
Because they can jump 'em

Why do gangstas like it when people's car batteries die?
Because they can jump 'em

So these golfing lawyers entered *a-Tourney*...

I tried to get my wet grass stains out in the *Lawn-Dry*.

Where does the best average golfer in the world place his car?
In the Par-King lot

My tree farm *Aspen* growing pretty well...

I'm not sure if all these sheep *Wool* stay warm...

—∞—

What is a cookie's favorite Disney movie?
Mulan-o

—∞—

I tried to return all my weapons, but I lost the *Warranty*.

—∞—

How much milk does a basketball player buy?
A Court

—∞—

I've always trusted my pencils; they've never *Led* me astray.

—∞—

I think I have cash, but let me *Check*...

—∞—

How did the student get to the college overseas?
On a Scholarship

So this bully left all of my grapes out to dry, for no good *Raisin.*

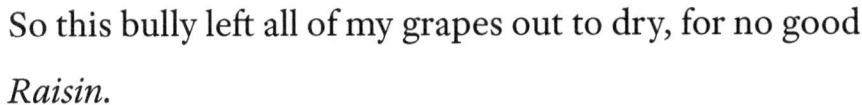

My talking cows are pretty annoying. They're always *Oxen* me questions...

My talking cows are pretty annoying. They're always *Oxen* me questions...

So this asthmatic gangsta girl was talking to *all-er-G's...*

So that Dutch music is pretty good, *Accordion* to me.

That pool table *Felt* pretty soft...

Why do wolves go to church so much?
So they can Prey

I just *Soldier* weapons for a pretty good price…

—⚏—

What do you call a super powered insect that can't talk?
A Mute-Ant

—⚏—

What is the rain's favorite dog?
A Poodle

—⚏—

I'm not allowed to be outside, so I guess I'll have to *Indoor*….. (Inside joke)

—⚏—

The cattle are doing pretty well this season, or so I've *Herd*…

—⚏—

The score between the oceans is *Tide*, but they both *Reef-use* to quit.

The score between the detergents is *Tide*,
Soap-osably...

—⁓—

So the score between the shoelaces is tied...apparently
they're having some *Is-shoes*

—⁓—

What is the most religious vehicle?
A Prius-t

—⁓—

So I was a *Speaker* at some stereo convention...

—⁓—

So I was a *Spoke-sman* for that bicycle convention...

—⁓—

Military ranks are pretty cool, in *General*...

What does a monkey cook his food on?
A Gorill-a

—◊—

I'm *Pressure* this tire is inflated enough...But I haven't *Tread* to see.

—◊—

Did you hear that short court trial about luggage? Yeah, it was a *Briefcase*...

—◊—

You didn't get that new furniture piece yet? Well, you *Ought-a-man*...

—◊—

I'm pretty tired from all this writing. I'm going to need to take a *Wrist*...

—◊—

I took my boots back; they had too many *is-Shoes*...

I think I'm headed toward the beach, but I'm not *Shore*...

—∞—

So the army officer was all, "Whose field bombs are these?" And I'm like, "Oh, those are *Mine*."

—∞—

I'll wait until the mountain gets warmer before I *Climate*.

—∞—

When my contractor finished my roof I was like, "How much is this going to cost?" and he said, "Oh, it's on the house!"

—∞—

Do you prefer your apples boiled, *Orchard*?

—∞—

What is a lumberjack's favorite month?
Sep-Timber

What is a NASCAR driver's favorite fruit?
Cherries, because of all the Pits

—∞—

Did you hear? The drycleaners just *Clothesed* down.

—∞—

What do you call a tangled rope in space?
An Astronaut

—∞—

Why didn't the astronaut pass training?
He was always Spacin' out

—∞—

How did the moon know that the sun liked him in the morning?
It always had Horizon him...

—∞—

They're making a theatrical production about broken bones. It has a pretty good *Cast*...

My insect trap is working pretty well, but it still has a few *Bugs*...

—◠◡—

I'm not sure what track and field sport to do; I'll need to *Discus* it with my coach.

—◠◡—

These twins smell pretty good, I bet they wear a lot of the same *C'lone*...

—◠◡—

So that paper for English was pretty *Essay*...

—◠◡—

So this thief was just *Ray-Ban* this sunglass store...

—◠◡—

How did the lumberjack get hurt?
In an Axe-ident

The pictures of my farm are a little too big; I'll need to *Crop* them...

—⁂—

I need to go to court for stealing headphones... my *Hearing* is today...

—⁂—

So these scientists keep wanting to experiment on my brain, but I don't *Mind*...

—⁂—

I finally found my world map, *Atlas*!

—⁂—

My new wooden chair has some good *Lumber* support...

—⁂—

That one wide receiver just got married. He had a pretty nice *Reception*...

Why couldn't the hose run in a race?
It Spray-nged its ankle

—w—

What brand of snacks does a female greeter serve?
Hostess

—w—

These chips went bad, but I'll *Stale* eat them.

—w—

How do stallions know how they're month is going to go?
Through their Horse-scope

—w—

Who do you hire to plant flowers in the ground?
A Floor-ist

—w—

So I've been *Pondering* about small lakes...

Why did the mattress thief stop stealing?
He was Cot

—∞—

What did the boom box say to the dog?
"Sup-Woofer"

—∞—

Before we close this nutrition shop, everything *Muscle*...

—∞—

If you don't take good care of your drums, there will be some *re-Percussions*...

—∞—

How did Snoop Dogg get down the mountain?
He Rap-eled

—∞—

So I *Thawwwwwwwwwww*-t my ice melted...

Where does a French man like to bungee jump?
Off the High-Fall tower

—ᴍ—

Why didn't getting hit with the soda bottle hurt?
Because it's a Soft-Drink!

—ᴍ—

Why was everyone slipping in ancient Rome?
Because of all the Greece

—ᴍ—

What is the ocean coasts' favorite sport?
Gulf

—ᴍ—

Why wasn't there air conditioning in the old days?
It wasn't *in-Vent-ed* yet

—ᴍ—

So the physician asked me to file some things. And I'm like,
"*Doc,-u-ment* these papers, right?"

Why was the hotel owner so sick?
He had too many Suites

—◊—

I can speak bird, *Flew-ently*.

—◊—

So whenever I'm feeling stressed, I listen to Jamaican music, to *Reggae-n* my repose.

—◊—

I'm having a birthday party the month after July. You can come, as *August*.

—◊—

What are glaciers' favorite hair styles?
A-Froze

—◊—

What did the surfer bully say to the annoying kid?
"I'm going to Beach you up."

What branch of the military did the horse join?
The Neighhhhh-vy...

—⚊—

Why do monkeys like the military so much?
Because of all the Branches

—⚊—

How does a gun like his hair cut?
With Bangs

—⚊—

This mean cop wouldn't help me... I even said *Police*.

—⚊—

Those covers they have for sewers are pretty *Grate*.

—⚊—

What happened to the construction worker who took extra supplies?
He was Build...

What is the most tranquil vegetable?

Peas

—◊—

What is a soda's dream job?

A Fizz-asist..........Pop star

—◊—

What is a Roman feline's favorite insect?

A Cat-a-Pillar

—◊—

Is that guy in the tropical flower garden a man, *Orchid*?

—◊—

So I was *Petal-ing* my flower bike...

—◊—

My friend just found out her clothes were too small. She threw a *Fit*.

So I wasn't sure when to drive through this intersection at a stoplight in Mexico. Then everyone was like, "*Green-Go!*"

—m—

So this dish was being disrespectful. I told him to be more *Plate...*

—m—

Did you see that guy with really bad acne? *Pore* guy...

—m—

So my friend wanted ashes from far away... I'll have to *Cinder* some

—m—

Where does a congressman store his cups?
In a Cabinet

—m—

What do you call two mallards that can't swim?
A Paradox

If I don't turn down the bass, I'm going to get in *Treble*...

—⁓—

What is an Indians currency's favorite shell?
A Scal'p

—⁓—

So these lazy pigs are pretty *Boar-ing*...

—⁓—

Wise this guy so smart?

—⁓—

What is the wealthiest part of a river?
The Banks

—⁓—

What is the most comfortable part of a river?
The Bed

Ever since I got lung problems, I haven't been able to breathe *Asthma-ch...*

—∞—

I just completed building this cool storage unit...for dogs. You *Shed* have seen it.

—∞—

What do you call a napping construction worker?
A Dozer

—∞—

Paying this debt all by myself has gotten pretty *Loan-ly...*

—∞—

That pig just got slaughtered, *Pork-guy.*

—∞—

So the math theatrical production is holding *Additions...*

Where does soap go to drink?
The Bar

—⁜—

Why didn't the potato want to go into the hot oil?
It was Fry-tend

—⁜—

What do you call the end of a frozen street?
A Cold-esac

—⁜—

Which Winnie the Pooh character is the best listener?
Eeyor

—⁜—

So I asked my Jewish friend, "*Yamaka* cap for me yet?"

—⁜—

What did the plant record music on?
Vine-el

That one blood filtering organ is pretty funny...just *Kidney-ing*.

—⦿—

So I was *Surgeon* for a doctor to operate on me...

—⦿—

So this photographer always *Lens* me his camera...

—⦿—

What is a Mexican chef's favorite thing to wear?
Flan-nels

—⦿—

What do you call someone who habitually hides their drugs on the roof?
An Attic-d

—⦿—

So I was selling poems, and this guy is like, "*Alibi* it!"

chapter 5

Which type of tree shows people to their chairs?
Cedar

—⁂—

Do you know how *Ferrari* have to drive...?

—⁂—

So I thought there was an opening in the ground, but I was just *Hole-ucinating*...

—⁂—

I want to be on the audience of Oprah, so I can *Winfrey* stuff.

—⁂—

What do you call a bunch of trashy books on the ground?
Litter-ature

—⁂—

All this painful Wattage *Hertz*...

So when the waiter didn't receive any money from the costumers, he was like, "It's pretty *Tip-ical*"

—ɯ—

So I was playing cards on my *Deck*...

—ɯ—

Did you read about that hanging in the *Nuece-paper*?

—ɯ—

-"So tomorrow is Thomas Edison's birthday..."
-"Really? *Wattage* will he be?"

—ɯ—

Where can you sing questions?
Inquire

—ɯ—

I wanted to learn about bikes, so I looked them up in the *en-Cycle-lo-Pedal-lia*...

I don't think I can get the bird you want, but *Owl* see what I can do.

—⚋—

What ethnicity ended the European war?
Finish

—⚋—

So I was supposed to *Meat* my butcher...

—⚋—

What happened to the bandit who stole phones in the Old West?
He was Hung up

—⚋—

So I just got some pickles for a pretty good *Dill*...

—⚋—

I guess I do have a pretty big house, now that you *Mansion* it.

So I was *Rum-aging* through this pirate's
liquor...

—⁓—

What part of the leg lets you know if it's sick?
The s-Neeze

—⁓—

My friend got a condiment in his eye, that *Must-hurt*.

—⁓—

What country can you buy a vehicle made of flowers?
Car-nation

—⁓—

Which ocean is most detailed?
The s-Pacific

—⁓—

Dis-guise not who you think he is...

Did you hear? Those zity prisoners just broke out!

—⁂—

That's aluminum! You can't *Foil* me.

—⁂—

The guy who won the no tooth-brushing contest got a *Plaque*...

—⁂—

What type of poem do you need to read on your feet?
A Stanza

—⁂—

What is a mountain climber's favorite type of poem?
A Hike-u

—⁂—

What is Shakespeare's favorite fruit?
A Poem-agranit

What is a boulder's favorite fruit?

A poma-Granite

—⁂—

So I'm doing this play about the alphabet and the 17th letter is like, "That's your Q!"

—⁂—

The people in that business meeting are too selfish...no one *a-Greed*.

—⁂—

The tube that goes down to the stomach is pretty *a-Soft-I-Guess...*

—⁂—

When I coughed up a baseball, my coach told me to *Throat*.

—⁂—

Lemons are pretty low on the pH scale, *Sour* limes.

Meet you on Thursday... you bring the water.
("That's a pretty week joke.")

—∞—

I eat that spicy chicken, *o-Cajun-ally*.

—∞—

What is the most argumentative sea animal?
Coral

—∞—

They are building a new zoo, *An-a-mall*...

—∞—

What is the sleepiest water activity?
Snore-kling

—∞—

How did dogs travel across the plains?
In a Wagon

My friend said we needed a torch to cut these metal brackets, and I'm like, "*Well-Der*!"

—⁊⁊—

Macaroni is the special next month, according to my *Colander*...

—⁊⁊—

So these lanterns are pretty *Light*...

—⁊⁊—

I was going to cook my own eggs at the restaurant, but *Omelet* the waiter do it.

—⁊⁊—

Did you hear that one male horse was elected *Mare*?

—⁊⁊—

I can now watch Horse television, thanks to my *Saddle-lite*...

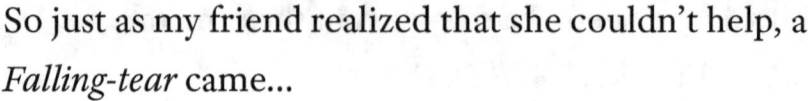

So just as my friend realized that she couldn't help, a *Falling-tear* came...

—ᴙ—

So I got *Cotton* this fluffy bush...

—ᴙ—

I want to eat all this food, but it *Stomach*.

—ᴙ—

I think I'll audition for that singing job. It seems like a great *Opera-tunity*...

—ᴙ—

So this dried plumb was *Pruning* bushes...

—ᴙ—

I cant recall, *Heavy* weighed that yet?

—ᴙ—

Worships supposed to sail to church today?

So lately, brain cells have been on my *Mind*...

—⚏—

What do you call a hundred year old plant?
A cen-Tree

—⚏—

I usually cook with a pot, but it *de-Pans*...

—⚏—

So this whale *Breached*...security.

—⚏—

So I was walking on the beach when I got *Sandal* in my shoe.

—⚏—

I just drove a couple thousand miles, now my car is pretty *Tired*...

—⚏—

Which farm animal can see in the dark?
A Lamb-p

What animal always wears flannels?

A Plaid-apus

—※—

What is a tree's favorite candy?

Twigs

—※—

My birthday card to the knife came late... It was *Beladed*...

—※—

What do you call a puzzle knife that dances?

A Jig-saw

—※—

So I was *Organ-izing* these church pianos...

—※—

So this lunar cow was *Mo'on*...

So at my store, I just *Salt* these spice grains...

—⋙—

I want to go to the concert, but I'm *Band*...

—⋙—

I want to go have a drink with the other excavators, but I'm a *Miner*...

—⋙—

I missed that story about the business prices, could you *Retail* it?

—⋙—

I wrote down when I'm going to draw in my *Sketch-ule*...

—⋙—

What color is always smiling?
Grin

What is a quad's favorite thing to watch?
A,TV

———⚏———

My friend got a public speaking *a-Word*...

———⚏———

So I was teaching my *Pupils* how to see...

———⚏———

Where does the mist get his money from?
The Fog bank

———⚏———

The catchers glove is pretty cool, I'll *ad-Mitt*.

———⚏———

I just started a new *Chip-ter* in this potato book...

———⚏———

"Have you ever watched that governmental council?"
"Yeah, I've *Senate*."

So this musical farmer just *Compost* a song...about soil.

—⁓—

So I was *Rifle-ing* through this gun ammunition *Magazine*...

—⁓—

So I went to this stylish pond to go *Fashion*.

—⁓—

My Hispanic friend *S'pain* to his home country many times...

—⁓—

When I had my store's grand opening, I didn't think anyone would Sh'op...
(Say Aloud)

—⁓—

I drove with some friends who have arthritis through this *Car-pool* tunnel...

My boss asked me, "Did you make those muscles yet?" and I'm like, "Yeah, I got *Tendon*."

—⸙—

I went fishing and *Cod* a lot...

—⸙—

So this international athlete just hurt his leg. Now he's *o-Limpian*.

—⸙—

Which body infection always helps out?
A-Cyst

—⸙—

My mad boss will be back soon. In the *Meantime*...

—⸙—

What did the surfer bull yell?
Cowabunga!

So I bet that the Catholic leader is pretty *Pope-ular*...

—m—

Sins when was there so much evil?

—m—

I'm not allowed to bake the bread into balls. Its against the *Rolls*.

—m—

So this rancher just *Goat* a new lamb...

—m—

So this dwarf was just *Nome-inated* as president...

—m—

What is a dwarf's favorite month?
Nome-vember

—m—

So this cold dwarf's hands went *Nome'b*...

Ever since the bad sailors attacked the bakery, *Pie-rates* have been skyrocketing.

—⚏—

So the price of space shuttles has been *Skyrocketing...*

—⚏—

What do you call a disobedient, tangled rope?
Naughty

—⚏—

So I have this yoga joke... But it's kind of a *Stretch.*

—⚏—

Yoga to that stretching class too?

—⚏—

Why is there so much controversy in the Bible?
Because of all the verses...

What kind of birds fly through canals?
Ducts

—⚮—

Which letter always waits in lines?
Queue

—⚮—

Which hotel do Mexican bands stay at?
The Marriot-chi

—⚮—

I asked this quarterback if he wanted to eat a football, but
he said that *he'd Pass.*

—⚮—

What is a peasant's favorite thing to do?
Serf

—⚮—

What do you call a normal torn shirt on a battlefield?
A Casual-T

So this Asian cook was like, "Let me *Shoyu* chicken..."

—◊—

So my job at the jewelry shop is pretty *Diamond-ing*...

—◊—

So when I saw this guy with no hair, I *Bald*...

—◊—

What is an umpire's favorite species of animal?
Fowl

—◊—

How much did the belt cost?
A Buck-le

—◊—

That blouse doesn't fit me anymore, it's too *Shirt*...

—◊—

So I just dropped all the roses all over the *Flower*...

What is a King's favorite writing utensil?
A Crown

—॥॥—

What is Crayola's favorite fruit?
Crayon-berry

—॥॥—

That guy was singing that church song really well, did you hear *Hymn*?

—॥॥—

What did the mischievous hiker do to his car windows?
He Tented them...

—॥॥—

That air conditioning festival was quite an e-*Vent*.

—॥॥—

That lady is being *Quiet* silent...

—॥॥—

Have you bought those dentures yet?
Yeah, I *Jaws*-t got them!

It was the end of the chickens shift, so he *Clucked* out...

—⚬—

The sport of fencing is pretty cool, if you're in to that *Sword* of thing...

—⚬—

So I went plug shopping at this electrical *Outlet*...

—⚬—

I'm not real good at thinking on the spot, I need to *Improv*....

—⚬—

My Hispanic friend wanted to drive a crane, he had a Loco-Motive...

—⚬—

You're in that singing group?
Of *Chorus*!

So I was *Salon* a bottle of shampoo...

—∞—

What's the most violent musical insect?

Beat-le

—∞—

What's the most serious color?

Laugh-Ender

—∞—

I have a mom... *A-Parent-ly*

—∞—

What is a grandma spider's favorite hobby?

Arach-Nitt-ing

—∞—

So that metal leaf meal is pretty *Salad*...

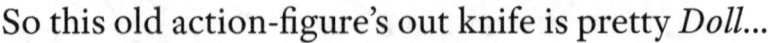

So this old action-figure's out knife is pretty *Doll*...

—⁜—

So this unfair cop just broke our car. He should *Bias* a new one...

—⁜—

*So I just punched this bug. I *Beet'le* be mad...

—⁜—

When the teacher played Beethoven for his students, it made the whole *Clas-sic*.

—⁜—

I didn't want to build that fence opening, but I was *obli-Gated*.

—⁜—

So I just saw this propane zombie... It was *Ghastly*.

—⁜—

I think that the Hobbits live over there, but I'm not *Shire*.

What is the smelliest mythical creature?
A Scent-aur

—⚡—

Which position in football always makes writing mistakes?
The White-Out

—⚡—

So I took this heavy dog to the *Pound*...

—⚡—

What type of ape always is talking on the phone?
An o-Rang-utang

—⚡—

When my friend left the stove on for too long, the room started to *Kitchen* fire...

—⚡—

So I asked this old rancher if there was anything that I could do *Farm*...

So when my friend saw me taking his farm house he was like, "What are you doing?!" and I'm like, "Oh, I'm just *Barn* it..."

—∞—

These bushes aren't *Foli-aged*...

—∞—

What is the funniest horse?
A Pun-ny

—∞—

My Jamaican friend asked when the hurricane was coming, and I'm like, "*Mon-soon.*"

—∞—

My friend bought this expensive Halloween outfit, I didn't think it would *Costume* that much.

—∞—

This girl asked me which of the two kiosks to go to, and I'm like "*Booth.*"

I'm looking for my cellular device. Oh! I just *Phoned* it.

—⚡—

I just *Medical* doctor...

—⚡—

My family just had an argument on what to eat. It was a *Fued*...

—⚡—

What's a bear's favorite Star Wars character?
Darth Maul

—⚡—

I wrote a song about baseball gloves, it's pretty *Catchy*.

—⚡—

That curvy road isn't so *Street*...

—⚡—

Have you ever *Scene* that one section of the movie?

Have you ever *Banana* fruit boat?

—⟋⟍—

I'm pretty stressed from looking at my wrist watch. I need to *Rolex*.

—⟋⟍—

Are you able to go to that African jungle?
Yeah, I Congo.

—⟋⟍—

To do the gallon challenge you need to be pretty *Dairy-ng*.

—⟋⟍—

I ordered cologne in the mail, it just *Scent*.

—⟋⟍—

What's the most enjoyable mythical creature?
Fawn

Why were Adam and Eve never hungry?
They were always Eden.

—⚯—

Where do truthful birds lay their eggs?
Honests

—⚯—

What does a Chinese chef do to exercise?
Wok

—⚯—

I set this wall up in the wrong place. I'll need to *Brick* it down.

—⚯—

My friend asked me if I've ever climbed any mountains made out of bones. I'm like, "Yeah! I *Skeleton* of them."

My lawn is pretty damp, *Moist* of the time...

—◊—

My friend is scared of climbing mountains, but *Hill* get over it.

—◊—

So this couple is *Wedding* to be married...

Sooo ... I was sailing across the sea with my Vessel, (just after giving blood).

And the ship started leaking, so my Seal patched that up.

Then the Skippy started to tear up the deck (cause he was Board I guess).

And I was like, "Mast you do that?"

But by that time, the seal had broken and the whole boat wasn't so Ship-shape anymore.

Then the captain got Anchory.

He told all of us, "Eye-patch that up if I was you!"

Then a bunch of fish beasts hopped aboard and started to take over; it was Mutant-y.

They were like, "We will destroy this boat!" And I begged them to Wreck-consider.

After that, they Whaled the guy standing next to me.

That's when I decided to High-Tail it out of there.

So then I arrived on an island. I was hungry. But the natives didn't grow tro-Pickle fruits.

Then while searching through the jungle, I found a supermarket employee out of Cash-Sheer luck.

I asked him, "Does this island Produce any fruit?"

He told me, "No, sorry pal. No produce here, but why don't you try the next Isle."

www.ingramcontent.com/pod-product-compliance
Lightning Source LLC
Chambersburg PA
CBHW060646130626
46555CB00002B/983